Disney · PIXAR

Disney PRESS

New York

Andy was a young boy with a big imagination. He loved playing with all his toys, but his favorite was a cowboy doll named Sheriff Woody.

"Reach for the sky!" Woody said when Andy pulled his string. **"You saved the day again, Woody!"** shouted Andy as he put the toy in his room and headed outside to play.

Once Andy was out of sight, his toys came to life. Woody called an emergency meeting with the other toys. "Okay. One minor note here," he told them. **"Andy's birthday party has been moved to today."**

Andy's family was moving to a new house, so his mom had decided to have the party early this year.

Woody sent a group of Green Army Men downstairs with a
baby monitor to keep an eye out for new toys. The Green Army
Men hid and reported back to the others as each toy was opened.
Sarge's voice crackled over the speaker. **"Come in,
Mother Bird. Mom has pulled a surprise
present from the closet!"**

Moments later, Andy and his friends raced upstairs to his room with the new toy. "Look! The laser lights up!" shouted Andy as he put the toy on his bed and ran downstairs for birthday cake.

Woody approached the cool new toy. **His name was Buzz Lightyear.** "There has been a bit of a mix-up," Woody said to the space ranger. "This is my spot, see, the bed here."

Just then, Buzz pressed a button and wings popped out of his back. "To infinity and beyond!" he shouted as he leaped off the bed and landed in front of Woody.

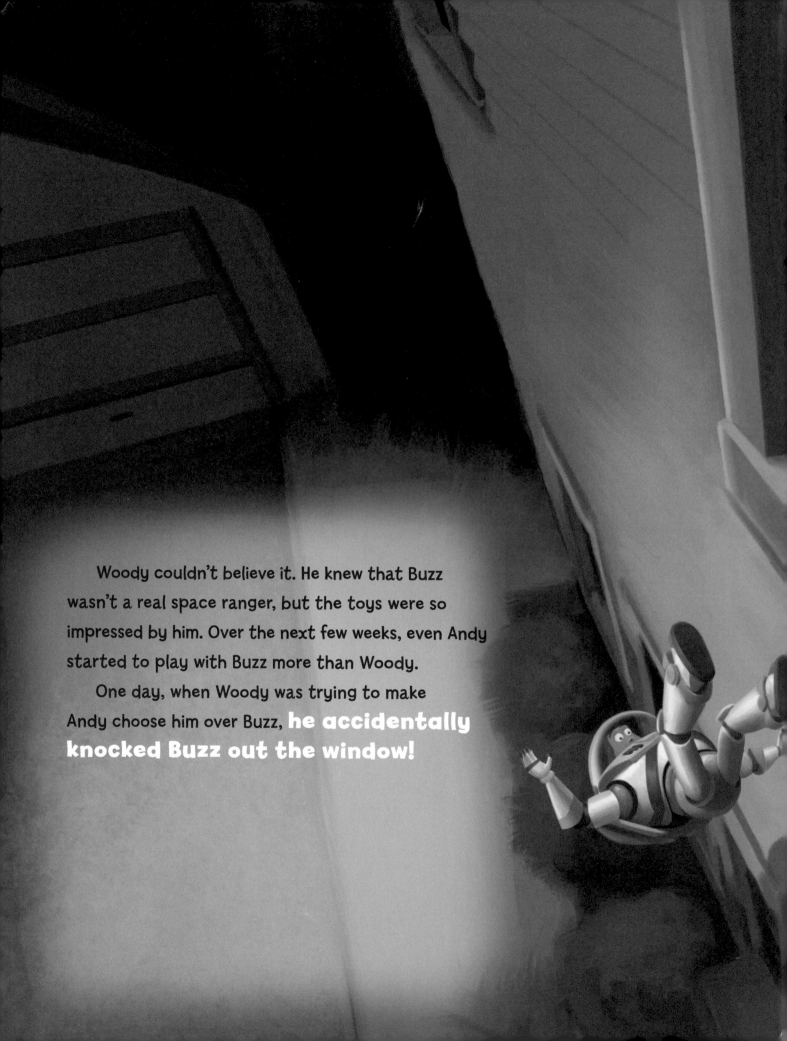

Woody couldn't believe it. He knew that Buzz wasn't a real space ranger, but the toys were so impressed by him. Over the next few weeks, even Andy started to play with Buzz more than Woody.

One day, when Woody was trying to make Andy choose him over Buzz, **he accidentally knocked Buzz out the window!**

Just then, Andy picked up Woody and carried him out to the van. Buzz raced after them and jumped inside.

Andy's family was headed to Pizza Planet, but on the way they stopped at a gas station. **Woody tried to explain to Buzz that he was a toy, but Buzz thought he was a real space ranger** with a mission to complete. The two of them got into a big fight and fell out of the van—just as it was driving away!

As Buzz stormed off, a Pizza Planet delivery truck pulled into the gas station. Woody convinced Buzz that the truck could help get him back to his planet, so the two climbed into the backseat.

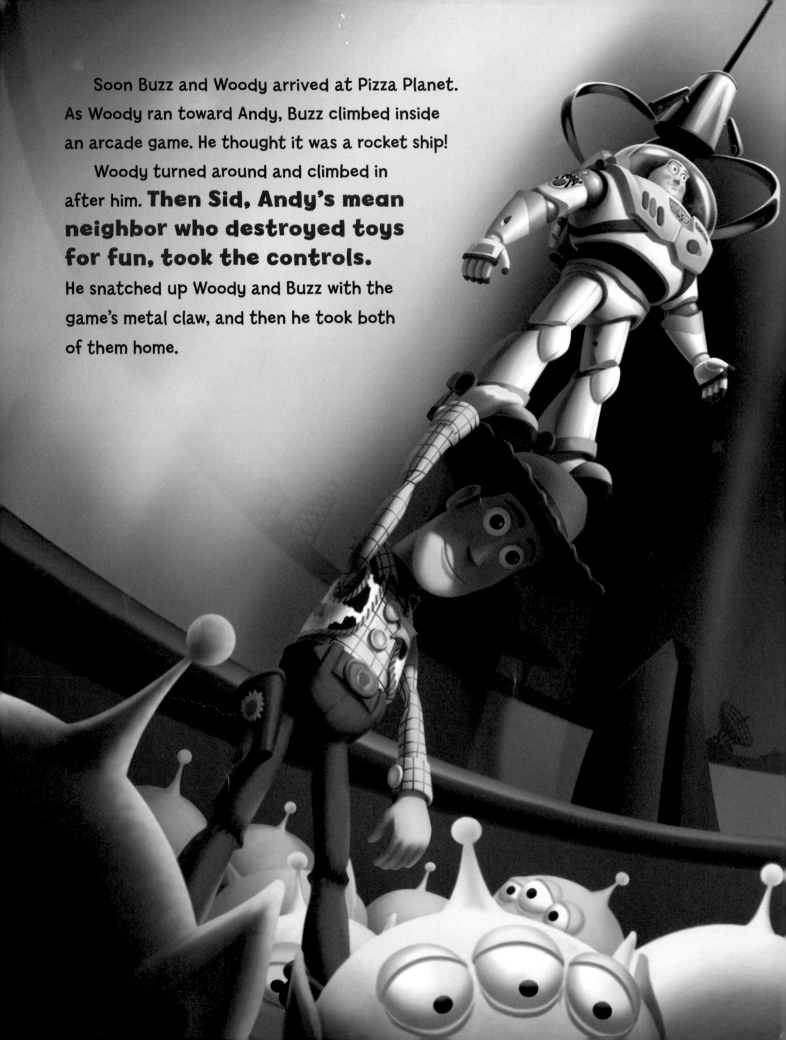

Soon Buzz and Woody arrived at Pizza Planet. As Woody ran toward Andy, Buzz climbed inside an arcade game. He thought it was a rocket ship!

Woody turned around and climbed in after him. **Then Sid, Andy's mean neighbor who destroyed toys for fun, took the controls.** He snatched up Woody and Buzz with the game's metal claw, and then he took both of them home.

Sid locked Buzz and Woody in his room. When they tried to escape, scary-looking toys blocked their way.

"Use your karate-chop action, Buzz!" shouted Woody.

Buzz pushed a button on his chest. **"Mayday! Mayday! Come in, Star Command! Send reinforcements!"** he cried.

But instead of attacking, the mutant toys crept back out of sight.

The next morning, Sid woke up
and went downstairs without locking
the door behind him. Woody and Buzz
quickly left the room.

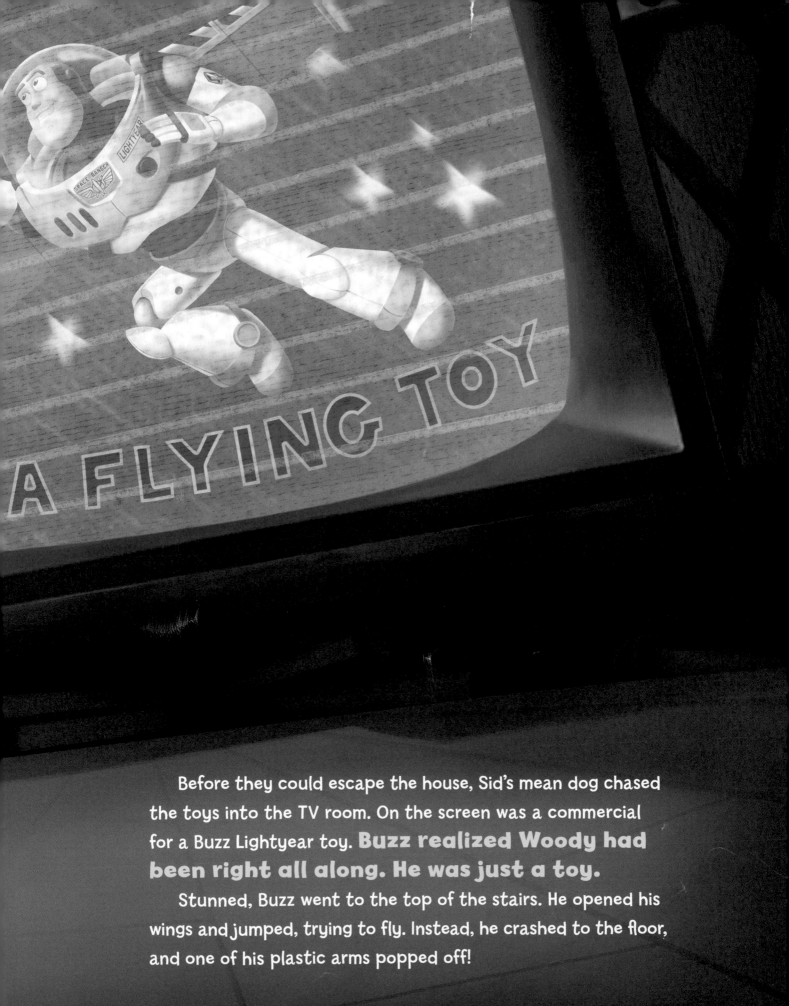

A FLYING TOY

Before they could escape the house, Sid's mean dog chased the toys into the TV room. On the screen was a commercial for a Buzz Lightyear toy. **Buzz realized Woody had been right all along. He was just a toy.**

Stunned, Buzz went to the top of the stairs. He opened his wings and jumped, trying to fly. Instead, he crashed to the floor, and one of his plastic arms popped off!

Woody found the one-armed Buzz. "Look at me. I can't even fly," Buzz said sadly.

Then Woody had an idea. The cowboy ran to Sid's window and called to the toys in Andy's room. **"Hey, guys! Guys!"** he yelled, waving Buzz's arm to get their attention.

But Woody held the arm too high. The others saw that it had been broken off. They thought Woody had hurt Buzz!

As they hurried away from the window, Woody called out. **"You've got to help us, please!** You don't know what it's like over here!"

All of a sudden, Sid's toys grabbed Buzz's
arm. They surrounded Buzz before Woody
could stop them.

When they backed away, Buzz's arm
was back in place! Woody was amazed.
"Hey . . . hey, they fixed you!"
he exclaimed.

Just then, Sid returned. He taped a giant rocket onto Buzz
and headed outside, but then it started to rain. Sid would have
to wait until tomorrow to set off the rocket.

That night while Sid slept, Woody begged Buzz to escape
with him and return to Andy. **But Buzz wouldn't move.
"I'm just a toy," he said quietly.**

Woody glared at Buzz. "Over there in that house is a kid who
thinks you are the greatest, and it's not because you're a space
ranger. It's because you're a toy. You are his toy!" argued Woody,
trying to cheer up Buzz.

The next morning, Sid's alarm clock rang. He jumped out of bed, grabbed Buzz, and ran outside.

Woody asked Sid's toys to help him save Buzz. The gang followed Sid and Buzz out to the yard.

Soon, Sid spotted Woody and picked him up. Then all of Sid's toys surrounded them. Woody looked right at the mean boy. "From now on," he said, **"you must take good care of your toys. Because if you don't, we'll find out."**

Woody's plan worked! Sid was scared. He ran into the house screaming. All the toys cheered!

The cowboy and space ranger couldn't celebrate for long. Next door, Andy's family and their moving truck were leaving. If they didn't hurry, they would be left behind! Woody and Buzz raced after the truck.

Buzz was able to climb on board. Woody was right behind him, but **Sid's dog, Scud, grabbed Woody with his teeth.** Buzz jumped off the truck to save him, but now Buzz was left behind with Scud!

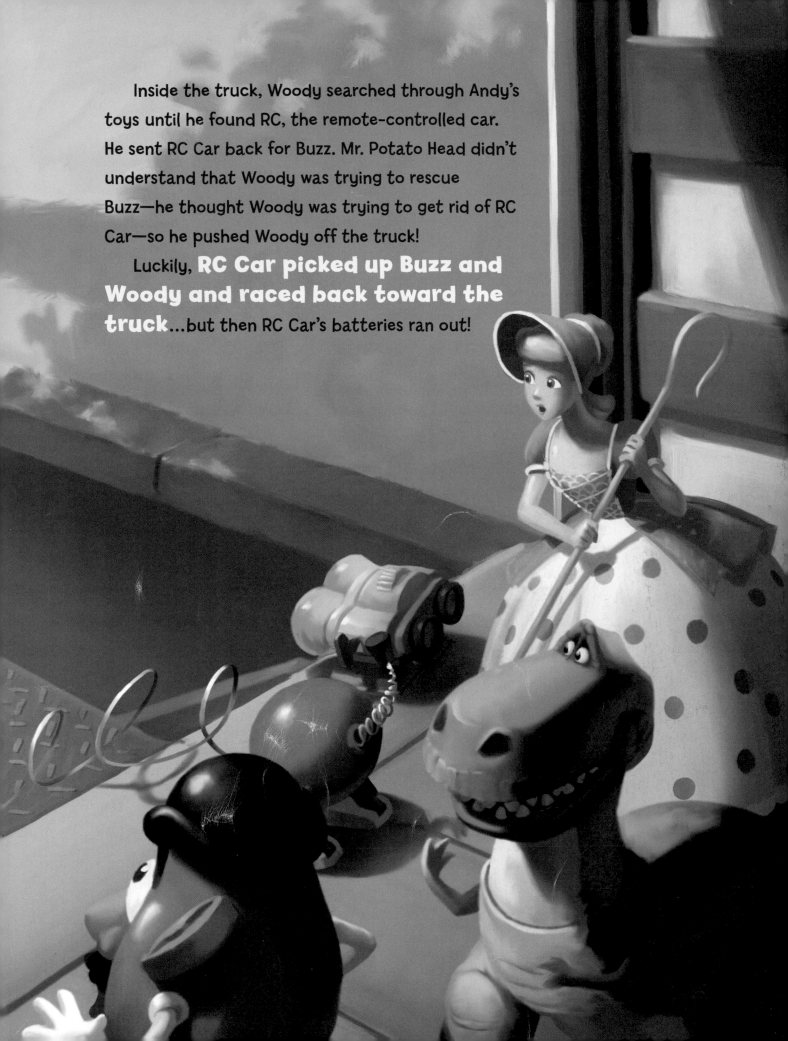

Inside the truck, Woody searched through Andy's toys until he found RC, the remote-controlled car. He sent RC Car back for Buzz. Mr. Potato Head didn't understand that Woody was trying to rescue Buzz—he thought Woody was trying to get rid of RC Car—so he pushed Woody off the truck!

Luckily, **RC Car picked up Buzz and Woody and raced back toward the truck**...but then RC Car's batteries ran out!

Woody and Buzz had an idea. The cowboy lit the fuse on the rocket that was still attached to Buzz. The toys shot straight into the air! They dropped RC Car safely into the back of the truck.

Then Buzz popped open his wings, setting the rocket free before it could explode.

Woody was thrilled. **"Hey, Buzz, you're flying!"** he exclaimed.

The two toys glided down toward Andy's van. They fell through the open sunroof and into a box. When Andy turned around, he let out a happy yell.

"**Hey! Wow! Woody! Buzz!**" he shouted. He had missed his two favorite toys.

That Christmas, the toys listened as Andy opened his first present.

"Buzz Lightyear, you're not worried, are you?" Woody asked.

"Me? No! No, no. Are you?" replied Buzz.

"Now, Buzz, what could possibly be worse than you?" Woody said with a smile.

It was a puppy! The toys looked at each other. Their next adventure was about to begin.

At Kohl's, we believe the simple act of caring creates a sense of community. Thanks to people like you, over the past 10 years Kohl's Cares for Kids® has raised millions of dollars to support children in the communities we serve. Throughout the year, Kohl's sells special Kohl's Cares for Kids merchandise with 100% of the net profit benefiting children's health and education initiatives nationwide.

Kohl's Cares for Kids is our way of supporting our customers and improving children's lives. So when you turn the pages of this book, remember you're not only reading a fun-filled adventure, you're also helping make a difference in the life of a child.

For more information about Kohl's Cares for Kids programs, visit www.kohlscorporation.com.

Certified Fiber Sourcing
www.sfiprogram.org
PWC-SFICOC-260
FOR TEXT ONLY